GO QUIZ YOURSELF!

AROUND THE WORLD

IZZI HOWELL

WAYLAND

www.waylandbooks.co.uk

First published in Great Britain in 2020 by Wayland

Copyright © Hodder and Stoughton Limited, 2020

Produced for Wayland by
White-Thomson Publishing Ltd
www.wtpub.co.uk

Series Editor: Izzi Howell
Series Designer: Rocket Design (East Anglia) Ltd

HB ISBN: 978 1 5263 1278 5
PB ISBN: 978 1 5263 1279 2

MIX
Paper from
responsible sources
FSC® C104740

Wayland
An imprint of
Hachette Children's Group
Part of Hodder & Stoughton
Carmelite House
50 Victoria Embankment
London EC4Y 0DZ

An Hachette UK Company
www.hachette.co.uk
www.hachettechildrens.co.uk

Printed in Dubai

Picture acknowledgements:
Getty: PytyCzech 7t, moonery 27, JTSorrell 37c; Peter Bull: 32–33c; Techtype: 36t; Shutterstock: Top Vector Studio, Daria Riabets, SaveJungle, Spreadthesign and Merfin cover and title page, Lidiia Koval 4, Sudowoodo 5t, Reenya 5b, okili77 6, 8, 12, 14, 18 and 20, Malchev, Zvereva Yana, narak0rn, K.Kyere and LineTale 6–7b, Spreadthesign, Valeri Hadeev and SaveJungle, 77Ivan 7cl, Maquiladora 7cr, olegtoka, nimograf, Sky Designs, Red monkey and Chalintra.B 8–9b, Olleg 9t, Sentavio, Maquiladora, Shanvood, SaveJungle and Christiane Franke 9c, reuse from pages 6–9 10–11, Sentavio, Tomacco, VectoRaith and imdproduction 12–13b, Antikwar 13t, SaveJungle, Rhoeo, Maquiladora, Daria Riabets and Professional Bat 13c, Bluehousestudio, Sentavio, Chalintra.B, Alexander Ryabintsev and Red monkey 14–15b, Jesus Sanz 15t, Hennadii H, Pogorelova Olga, Giraffarte and Maria Siubar 15c, reuse from pages 12–15 16–17, Infinity Eternity, Sentavio, studioworkstock and SaveJungle 18–19b, Faya Francevna 19t, AnnstasAg, Gaidamashchuk, Nadya_Art, A7880S, iana kauri, HappyPictures and Maquiladora 19c, Nadya_Art, Dimec, A7880S and Genesis Parra 20–21b, saiko3p 21t, A7880S, Rhoeo, Eno Boy and GoodStudio 21c, reuse from pages 18–21 22–23, DidGason 24t, LANTERIA 24b, matrioshka 25t, A7880S 25b, Teresa Prokhoryan 26t, Peter Hermes Furian 26b, Sunnydream, Chonnanit, Rvector, Shanvood and KittyVector 27, reuse from pages 24–27 28–29, Yusiki 30, Midorie 31t, Natali Snailcat 31b, SaveJungle, Elegant Solution and joilaird 32, Lidiia, SaveJungle, Zvereva Yana, ActiveLines and Tikofff1 33, reuse from pages 30–33 34–35, Kseniya Art 36b, Arsgera 37t, Oceloti 37b, Zvereva Yana 38t, rudvi 38c, passengerz 38b, ActiveLines 38–39, Mascha Tace, Kaewta and Nadya_Art 39, reuse from pages 36–39 40–41, all_is_magic 42t, Studio Ayutaka 42c, whyt 42b, lady-luck 43t, Maryna Yakovchuk 43c, Blan-k 43b, Lidiia Koval 45, reuse from book 46–47.
All design elements from Shutterstock.

The website addresses (URLs) included in this book were valid at the time of going to press. However, it is possible that contents or addresses may have changed since the publication of this book. No responsibility for any such changes can be accepted by either the author or the publisher.

All population statistics were true at the time of print.

CONTENTS

HOW TO USE THIS BOOK

This book is packed full of amazing facts and statistics. When you've finished reading a section, test yourself with questions on the following page. Check your answers on pages 44–45 and see if you're a quizmaster or if you need to quiz it again! When you've finished, test your friends and family to find out who's the ultimate quiz champion!

CAVAN COUNTY

OUR WORLD

Planet Earth is our home. It is the only known place in the universe that contains life. People around the world in different countries have a wide range of cultures, identities, languages and religions.

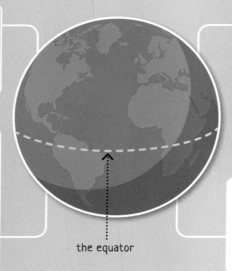

the equator

AROUND 70%
of Earth's surface is covered in water.

THE EQUATOR
divides Earth into two parts – the Northern Hemisphere and the Southern Hemisphere.

The equator is an imaginary line around the centre of Earth. It measures **40,075 km**.

The land on Earth is divided into **7 CONTINENTS**.

 GROWING NUMBERS In 10,000 BCE, the world population was 4 million.

WORLD POPULATION

The world population is 7.5 billion and growing. For most of human history, the population on Earth was low. However, as healthcare, food production and cleanliness improved, the population increased dramatically. If the world's population continues to grow in this way, we won't have enough resources to go around.

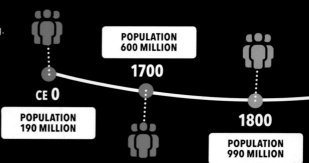

POPULATION 600 MILLION

1700

CE 0

POPULATION 190 MILLION

1800

POPULATION 990 MILLION

COUNTRIES

According to the United Nations, there are 193 countries on Earth. The newest country is South Sudan, which became independent in 2011. What is considered a country is a political issue. Some areas, such as Kosovo, would like to become their own country, but are not able to yet.

PEOPLE OF THE WORLD

The world is a diverse place, full of different habitats, animals, people, cultures and languages. It is important to learn about other people around the world and respect their way of life.

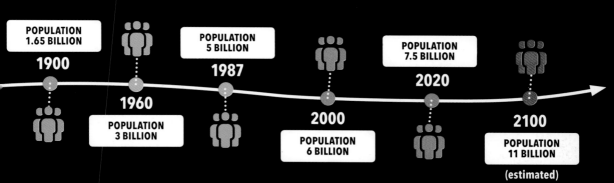

POPULATION 1.65 BILLION
1900

1960
POPULATION 3 BILLION

POPULATION 5 BILLION
1987

2000
POPULATION 6 BILLION

POPULATION 7.5 BILLION
2020

2100
POPULATION 11 BILLION
(estimated)

AFRICA

The continent of Africa covers about one fifth of the land on Earth. It stretches for 8,000 km from north to south, from the Mediterranean coast down to the bottom of South Africa.

Number of countries: **54**

Size: **30,365,000 square km**

Population: **1.3 billion**

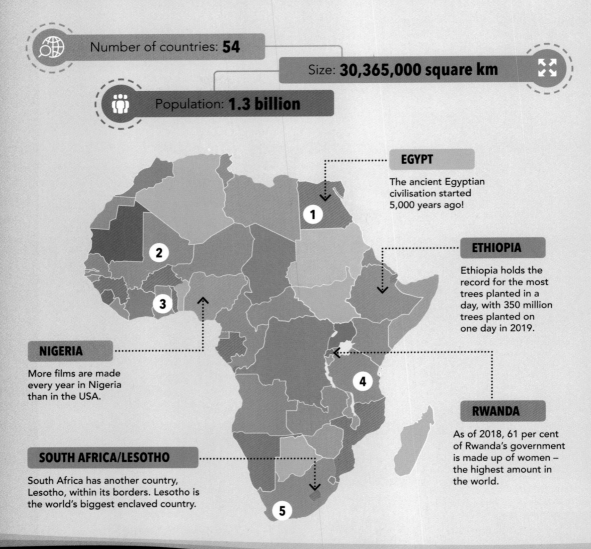

EGYPT

The ancient Egyptian civilisation started 5,000 years ago!

ETHIOPIA

Ethiopia holds the record for the most trees planted in a day, with 350 million trees planted on one day in 2019.

NIGERIA

More films are made every year in Nigeria than in the USA.

RWANDA

As of 2018, 61 per cent of Rwanda's government is made up of women – the highest amount in the world.

SOUTH AFRICA/LESOTHO

South Africa has another country, Lesotho, within its borders. Lesotho is the world's biggest enclaved country.

AFRICAN LANDMARKS

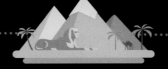

1 Pyramids of Giza, Egypt

2 Great Mosque of Djenné, Mali

THE EQUATOR

The equator runs through the centre of the continent, going through seven African countries. The area around the equator has a tropical, wet climate with areas of rainforest. To the north and the south of the equator are grasslands, known as savannah. Beyond the grasslands, there are dry deserts, such as the Sahara and the Kalahari.

DESERT

SAVANNAH

RAINFOREST

📇 *EARLY MAN*

Scientists believe that humans (*Homo sapiens*) first evolved in Africa around 315,000 years ago.

Archaeologists have found many remains of humans and early human ancestors in East Africa.

They studied these bones to understand how humans evolved.

The first humans migrated out of Africa and travelled across the world.

MEGA BEASTS

Africa is home to the world's tallest animal, the giraffe, and the largest land animal, the African bush elephant. The deadliest large land animal, the hippopotamus, is also found in Africa. Hippopotamuses are very aggressive and have sharp teeth.

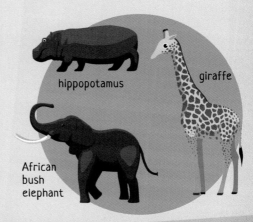

hippopotamus

giraffe

African bush elephant

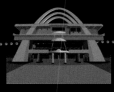

3 Black Star Square, Ghana

4 Mount Kilimanjaro, Tanzania

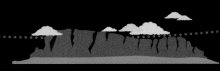

5 Table Mountain, South Africa

EUROPE

Europe is the second smallest continent. It is connected by land to Asia in the east. Europe stretches from Iceland and Scandinavia in the north to Greece, Italy and Spain in the south.

Number of countries: **50***

*(3 of which also have land in Asia)

Size: **10,000,000 square km**

Population: **750 million**

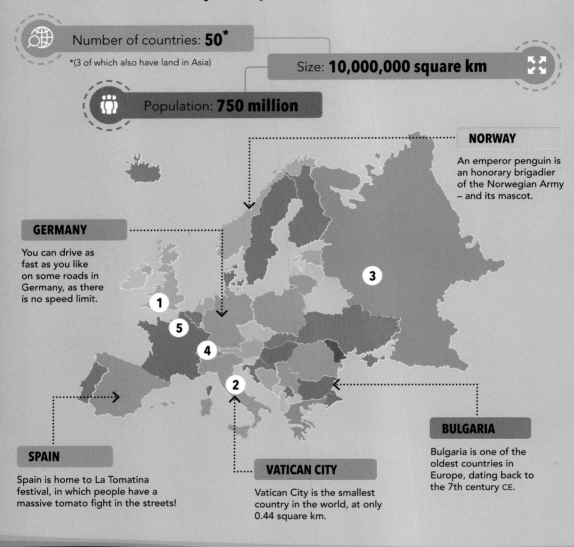

NORWAY

An emperor penguin is an honorary brigadier of the Norwegian Army – and its mascot.

GERMANY

You can drive as fast as you like on some roads in Germany, as there is no speed limit.

BULGARIA

Bulgaria is one of the oldest countries in Europe, dating back to the 7th century CE.

SPAIN

Spain is home to La Tomatina festival, in which people have a massive tomato fight in the streets!

VATICAN CITY

Vatican City is the smallest country in the world, at only 0.44 square km.

EUROPEAN LANDMARKS

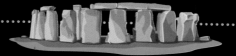

1 Stonehenge, the UK

2 The Colosseum, Italy

THE EUROPEAN UNION

Nearly thirty European countries are members of the European Union (EU). The EU was created to make it easier for European countries to trade with each other. Citizens of EU countries can move freely between any countries in the EU. Many EU countries use the same currency – the Euro.

the flag of the European Union

EUROPEAN WILDLIFE

As Europe and Asia are connected, many animals live on both continents as they can move freely back and forth. However, there are some animals that are unique to Europe.

pine marten

red kite

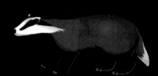

European badger

Iberian lynx

ANCIENT CIVILISATIONS

Europe was home to two massive ancient civilisations – ancient Greece and ancient Rome. The ancient Greeks introduced the world to democracy, the Olympic Games and philosophy. The ancient Romans developed the alphabet that is used in English and many other languages around the world, and built great buildings and roads.

the ancient Greek Acropolis in Athens, Greece

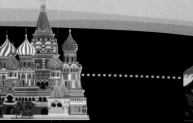

3 St Basil's Cathedral, Russia

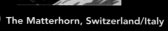

4 The Matterhorn, Switzerland/Italy

5 The Eiffel Tower, France

GO QUIZ YOURSELF!

1 How much of Earth's surface is covered in water?

2 How many continents are there on Earth?

3 What is the newest country?

4 What was the world population in 10,000 BCE?

5 What was the world population in 2020?

6 How many countries are there in Africa?

7 Which country is found within the borders of South Africa?

8 In which African country is Mount Kilimanjaro?

9 What is the climate like around the equator in Africa?

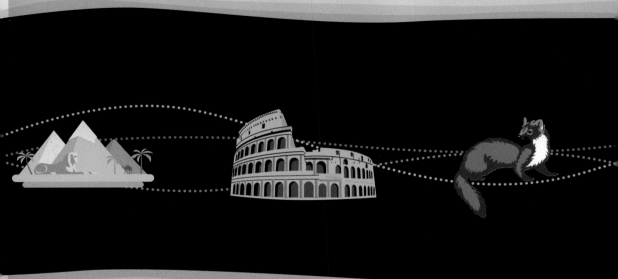

- - - -> **10** When did humans (*Homo sapiens*) first evolve in Africa?

11 Which African animal is the deadliest large land animal?

12 Which continent is Europe connected to?

13 How large is Europe?

14 Which European country is the smallest country in the world?

15 In which European country is the Colosseum found?

16 What is the shared currency of many EU countries?

17 Which ancient civilisation introduced democracy, philosophy and the Olympic Games to the world?

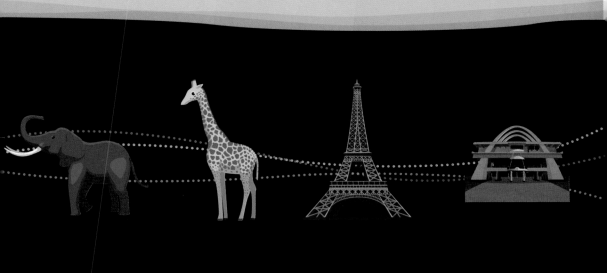

ASIA

Asia is the largest continent with the highest population. It occupies around one third of all land on Earth. Asia stretches from Turkey in the west to Indonesia and Japan in the east.

Number of countries: **48***

*(3 of which also have land in Europe)

Size: **44,614,000 square km**

Population: **4.7 billion**

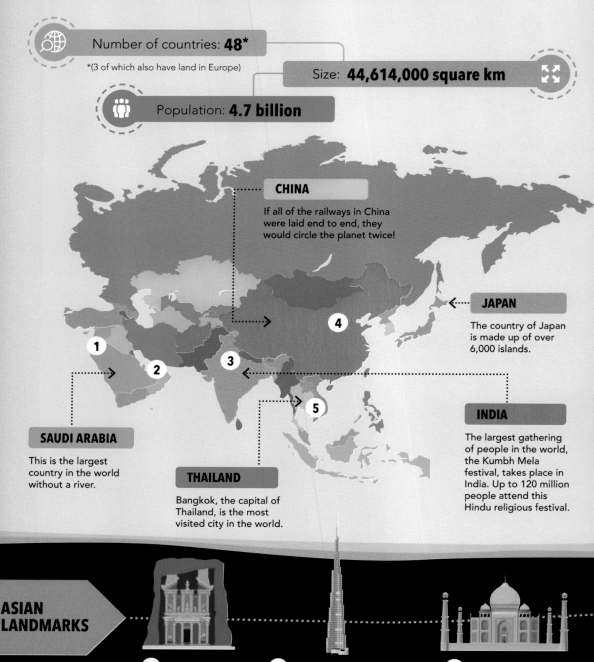

CHINA

If all of the railways in China were laid end to end, they would circle the planet twice!

JAPAN

The country of Japan is made up of over 6,000 islands.

INDIA

The largest gathering of people in the world, the Kumbh Mela festival, takes place in India. Up to 120 million people attend this Hindu religious festival.

SAUDI ARABIA

This is the largest country in the world without a river.

THAILAND

Bangkok, the capital of Thailand, is the most visited city in the world.

ASIAN LANDMARKS

1 Petra, Jordan

2 Burj Khalifa, Dubai, UAE

3 The Taj Mahal, India

PEOPLE AND POPULATION

Two of the largest countries in the world by population, China and India, are located in Asia. Both are home to over 1 billion people. The largest country in the world by size, Russia, is also mainly located in Asia, although some of its territory is also in Europe. Some of the smaller Asian countries by size, such as Singapore and Bangladesh, also have large populations, resulting in a high population density.

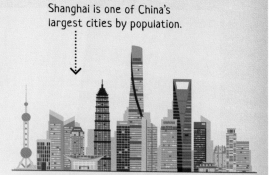

Shanghai is one of China's largest cities by population.

Mount Everest

HIGHS AND LOWS

Asia contains the highest and lowest points on Earth. The highest point is Mount Everest in the Himalayas, reaching 8,850 m above sea level. The lowest point on land is the Dead Sea, found in Israel and Jordan, which measures 430 m below sea level.

WILDLIFE

There are many different habitats in Asia, from the high mountains of the Himalaya to the rainforests of Southeast Asia and grassy plains of China. This has led to a diverse range of animal life, with many species that can only be found in Asia.

snow leopard in central Asia

orangutan on the islands of Sumatra and Borneo

tiger across parts of India, China, Russia and Southeast Asia

giant panda in China

king cobra in India and Southeast Asia

4 The Great Wall of China, China

5 Angkor Wat, Cambodia

OCEANIA

Oceania is made up of the islands of Australia, New Zealand and over 10,000 other islands in the Pacific Ocean, such as Fiji, Tahiti and Samoa. Australia is the largest and most-populated country in Oceania.

Number of countries: **15**

Size: **8,525,989 square km**

Population: **43 million**

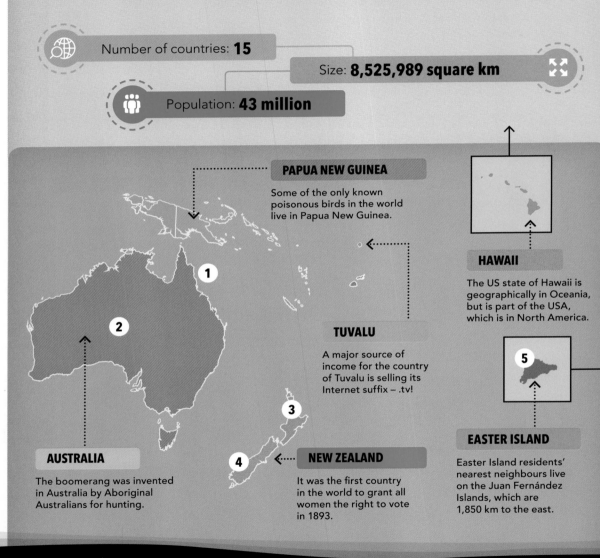

PAPUA NEW GUINEA

Some of the only known poisonous birds in the world live in Papua New Guinea.

HAWAII

The US state of Hawaii is geographically in Oceania, but is part of the USA, which is in North America.

TUVALU

A major source of income for the country of Tuvalu is selling its Internet suffix – .tv!

AUSTRALIA

The boomerang was invented in Australia by Aboriginal Australians for hunting.

NEW ZEALAND

It was the first country in the world to grant all women the right to vote in 1893.

EASTER ISLAND

Easter Island residents' nearest neighbours live on the Juan Fernández Islands, which are 1,850 km to the east.

OCEANIA LANDMARKS

 The Great Barrier Reef, Australia

 Uluru, Australia

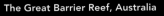

CITIES

The top ten largest cities in Oceania are all in Australia and New Zealand. Sydney, Australia, is the largest, with over 5.2 million people. The smaller, remote islands in Oceania tend to have smaller populations. People live in towns and villages, where the main industries are tourism and farming.

Sydney

PEOPLE

Before European people invaded countries in Oceania, there were many indigenous groups of people across the islands, such as the Māori in New Zealand and Aboriginal Australians. After the European invasion, a huge number of indigenous people were wiped out by disease. Land was stolen from them and they were forced to change their culture. Although people try to protect and celebrate these cultures today, indigenous people still face prejudice.

MARSUPIALS AND MONOTREMES

Oceania is home to a group of mammals called marsupials. These animals give birth to their young before they are fully developed. Marsupial young attach themselves to their mother, sometimes in a pouch, and drink her milk while they finish developing. It is also home to another unusual group of mammals called monotremes. These mammals lay eggs instead of giving birth to live young.

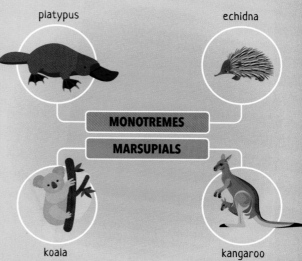

platypus

echidna

MONOTREMES

MARSUPIALS

koala

kangaroo

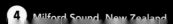

GO QUIZ YOURSELF!

18 What is the population of Asia?

19 Which Asian city is the most visited city in the world?

20 How many islands make up the country of Japan?

21 In which country is Angkor Wat?

22 What are the two largest countries in the world by population?

23 How tall is Mount Everest?

24 What is the lowest point on land on Earth?

25 Where do giant pandas live?

26 What is the largest country in Oceania by size?

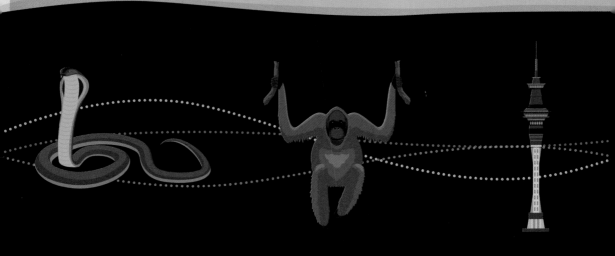

27 How many countries are in Oceania?

28 Which country in Oceania was the first to give all women the right to vote?

29 Who invented the boomerang?

30 Which US state is found in Oceania?

31 In which country are the Moai statues?

32 Which indigenous people live in New Zealand?

33 Name a marsupial.

34 How do monotremes have young, rather than giving birth to live young?

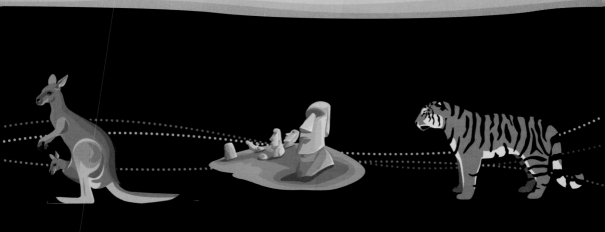

NORTH AMERICA

North America is the third largest continent. It stretches for 8,000 km from north to south, coming within 800 km of both the North Pole and the equator.

Number of countries: **23**

Size: **24,230,000 square km**

Population: **370 million**

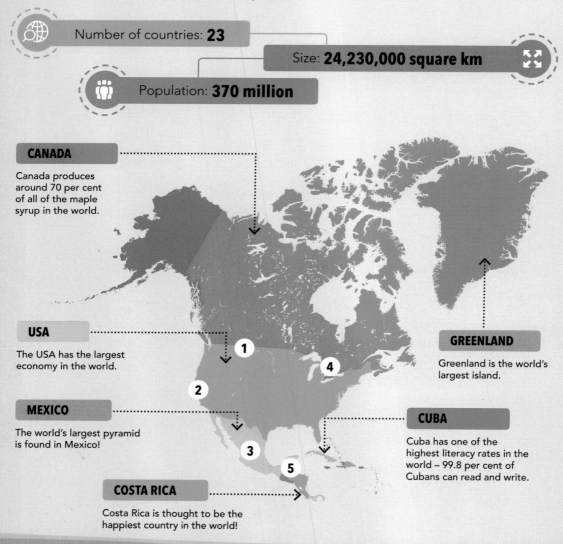

CANADA

Canada produces around 70 per cent of all of the maple syrup in the world.

USA

The USA has the largest economy in the world.

MEXICO

The world's largest pyramid is found in Mexico!

COSTA RICA

Costa Rica is thought to be the happiest country in the world!

GREENLAND

Greenland is the world's largest island.

CUBA

Cuba has one of the highest literacy rates in the world – 99.8 per cent of Cubans can read and write.

NORTH AMERICAN LANDMARKS

CITIES

Some of the largest cities on Earth are found in North America. Mexico City, the capital of Mexico, is the largest city in North America. In the USA, many people live in the huge cities of New York and Los Angeles.

New York

NORTH TO SOUTH

The north of the continent is close to the North Pole. This area has cold temperatures and ice and snow. As you move south, the most common habitats are forests and grassland (known as prairies). There are also areas of desert. Central America and the Caribbean islands have a tropical climate with rainforests.

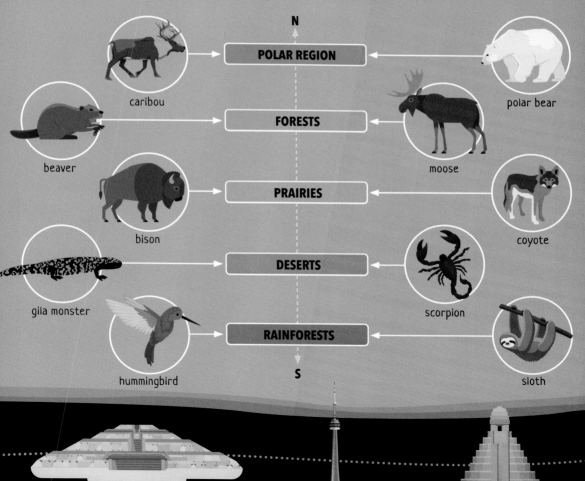

N

caribou

POLAR REGION

polar bear

beaver

FORESTS

moose

bison

PRAIRIES

coyote

gila monster

DESERTS

scorpion

hummingbird

RAINFORESTS

sloth

S

3 Pyramid of the Sun, Mexico

4 CN Tower, Canada

5 Tikal, Guatemala

SOUTH AMERICA

This continent is located to the south of North America. The two continents are connected by a land bridge that is just 82 km wide in some places. Apart from Antarctica, South America is the continent that reaches furthest south.

Number of countries: **23**

Size: **24,230,000 square km**

Population: **370 million**

VENEZUELA

Angel Falls, the world's highest uninterrupted waterfall, is in Venezuela.

ISTHMUS OF PANAMA

This land bridge connects South America to North America and it is the location of the country of Panama.

ECUADOR

The closest place on Earth to space, Mount Chimborazo, is found in Ecuador. This is because Earth bulges around the equator, so the land is higher here.

BRAZIL

The world's largest carnival takes place in Rio de Janeiro, Brazil. It attracts around 2 million visitors!

CHILE

The oldest mummies in the world were made in Chile in around 5,000 BCE, 2,000 years before the ancient Egyptians!

PERU

There are more than 6,000 different species of plants in 1 square km of Peruvian rainforest.

SOUTH AMERICAN LANDMARKS

1 Nazca Lines, Peru

2 Christ the Redeemer, Brazil

HABITATS

There are many different habitats across South America, including tropical rainforests, such as the Amazon, grasslands, known as pampas, and the high mountainous habitat on the Andes Mountains. It is so cold in the south of the continent that there are glaciers and penguins.

THE AMAZON RAINFOREST

The Amazon Rainforest covers around 6 million square km of South America in the river basin of the Amazon River. It is split between Brazil, Peru, Colombia and other surrounding countries. It is the most biodiverse area on Earth, with millions of species of plant, insect, bird, fish and mammal. Many species in the Amazon are yet to be discovered by scientists.

MACHU PICCHU

The remains of the Incan city of Machu Picchu are located in Peru.

The city is built at a height of 2,350 m in the Andes Mountains.

The Inca had a massive empire along the west coast of South America in the 15th and 16th centuries.

GREEN ANACONDA
near to water in tropical areas

VICUÑA
mountains

ELECTRIC EEL
freshwater around the Amazon River and the Orinoco River

TOUCAN
forests

Native animals

There are many different native species across South America, in each of its diverse habitats. Many of these species can't be found anywhere else in the world.

JAGUAR
rainforests, wetlands and grasslands

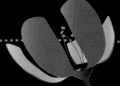

3 Floralis Genérica, Argentina (a metal

4 Torres del Paine National Park, Chile

GO QUIZ YOURSELF!

35 What is the population of North America?

36 Which North American country produces 70 per cent of the world's maple syrup?

37 In which North American country is the world's largest pyramid?

38 Which North American country is thought to be the happiest country in the world?

39 In which country is the Golden Gate Bridge?

40 What is the largest city in North America?

41 What is the climate like in the north of North America?

42 Name an animal that lives on the prairies of North America.

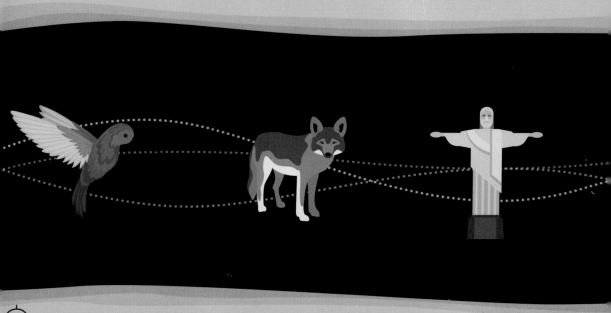

43 How wide is the narrowest point on the Isthmus of Panama – the land bridge between North and South America?

44 How many people attend the world's largest carnival in Rio de Janeiro, Brazil?

45 What is the name of the highest uninterrupted waterfall, which is found in Venezuela?

46 In which country is the statue of Christ the Reedemer?

47 What are the pampas?

48 How large is the Amazon Rainforest?

49 Which South American civilisation built the city of Machu Picchu?

50 How high is the city of Machu Picchu?

51 In which areas do green anaconda live?

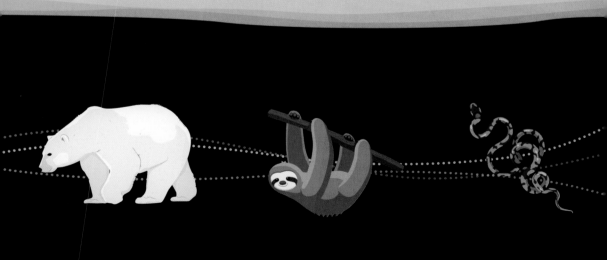

ANTARCTICA

The continent of Antarctica lies around the South Pole. It is almost entirely covered with ice.

Number of countries: **0**

Size: **14,200,000 square km**

Population: **0 permanent residents**

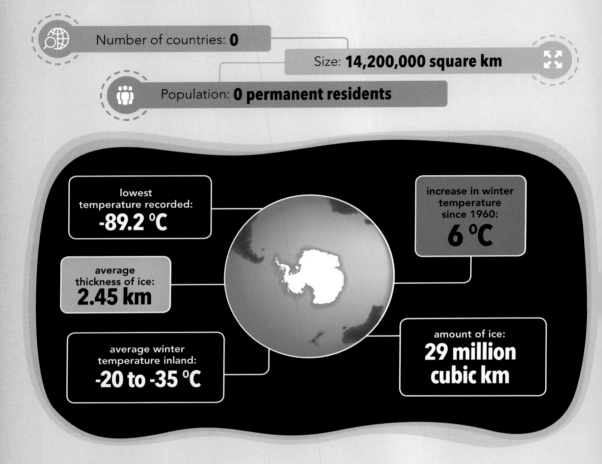

lowest temperature recorded:
-89.2 °C

average thickness of ice:
2.45 km

average winter temperature inland:
-20 to -35 °C

increase in winter temperature since 1960:
6 °C

amount of ice:
29 million cubic km

ICE AND LAND

Unlike the North Pole, there is land under the ice of Antarctica. This is why it is considered a continent. Some of this ice also extends out over the ocean, creating an ice shelf. A long chain of mountains runs through the centre of Antarctica. To the east, there is a high plateau and to the west are islands, which are hidden by the ice.

WHO'S IN CHARGE?

Antarctica does not belong to any country. In 1959, many countries signed a treaty agreeing that Antarctica should be made an area of scientific research for all nations. No armies, weapons or military bases are allowed. Drilling for oil on Antarctica is also forbidden.

SCIENTIFIC RESEARCH

Many different types of scientific research are carried out on Antarctica. Scientists live and work at research stations, usually just for part of the year. They study the climate, geology and wildlife of Antarctica. It is also a great location to study space, as there is little light or air pollution to block the view of the stars.

PLANTS AND ANIMALS

There aren't many plant species on Antarctica, other than lichens. There is a huge amount of life in the seas around Antarctica, including fish, whales and seals. A few species, such as penguins, live on the ice.

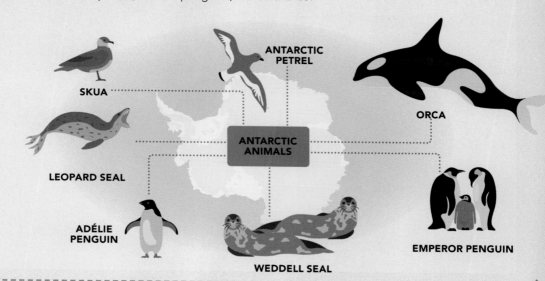

SKUA

ANTARCTIC PETREL

ORCA

LEOPARD SEAL

ANTARCTIC ANIMALS

ADÉLIE PENGUIN

WEDDELL SEAL

EMPEROR PENGUIN

CULTURE, LANGUAGE AND RELIGION

People around the world speak different languages, follow different customs, eat different food and follow different religions. This is all part of the rich tapestry that makes our planet so special.

LANGUAGES

Today, just over 7,000 languages are spoken on Earth. Some are used by millions of people, while others are spoken by just a handful. Languages around the world are written in different alphabets and in different directions (left to right, right to left, top to bottom). Many people speak more than one language.

MOST SPOKEN FIRST LANGUAGES

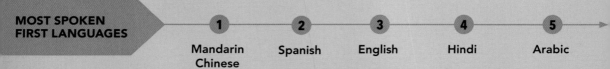

1	2	3	4	5
Mandarin Chinese	Spanish	English	Hindi	Arabic

RELIGION

Around 84 per cent of people consider themselves to be part of an organised religion. Some religions are more common in certain parts of the world. For example, 99 per cent of Hindus and Buddhists live in Asia. Over time the number of people who follow each religion changes. At the moment, Islam is the fastest-growing religion, followed by Christianity.

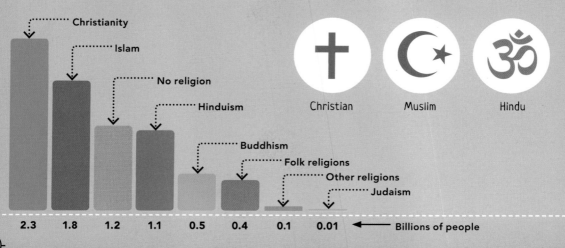

Christianity · Islam · No religion · Hinduism · Buddhism · Folk religions · Other religions · Judaism

Christian · Muslim · Hindu

| 2.3 | 1.8 | 1.2 | 1.1 | 0.5 | 0.4 | 0.1 | 0.01 |

← Billions of people

DELICACIES AROUND THE WORLD

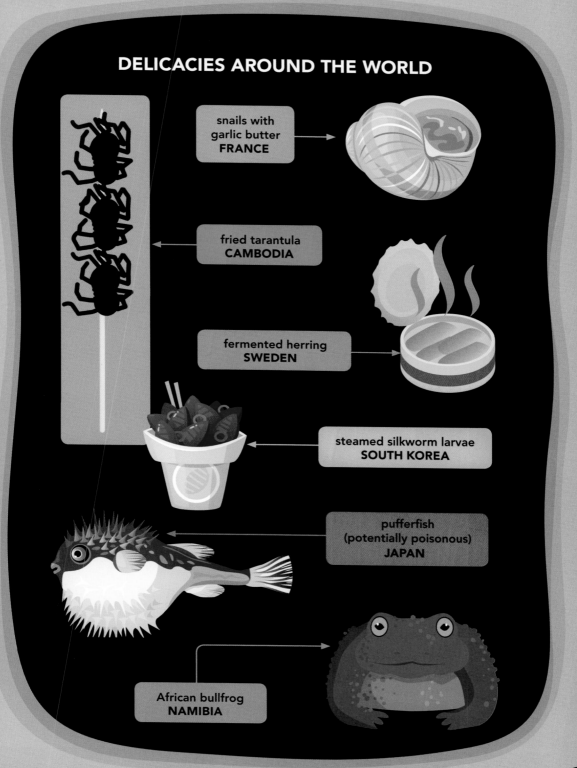

snails with garlic butter **FRANCE**

fried tarantula **CAMBODIA**

fermented herring **SWEDEN**

steamed silkworm larvae **SOUTH KOREA**

pufferfish (potentially poisonous) **JAPAN**

African bullfrog **NAMIBIA**

GO QUIZ YOURSELF!

52 What covers most of Antarctica?

53 How large is Antarctica?

54 What is the lowest temperature recorded on Antarctica?

55 What is the average ice thickness on Antarctica?

56 Where is the chain of mountains located on Antarctica?

57 Which country does Antarctica belong to?

58 Name something that is forbidden on Antarctica.

59 Why is Antarctica a good place to observe space?

60 Name a type of penguin that lives on Antarctica.

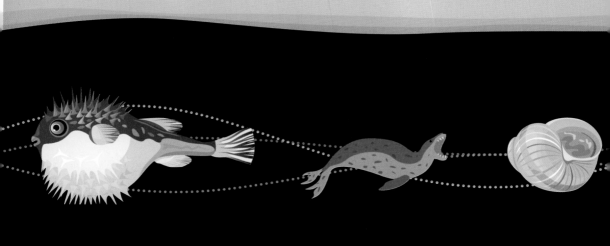

61 How many languages are spoken on Earth?

62 What is the most spoken first language?

63 What percentage of people consider themselves to be part of an organised religion?

64 On which continent do 99 per cent of Hindus live?

65 How many people are Christians?

66 Which religion has half a billion followers around the world?

67 In which country are fried tarantulas eaten?

68 Why is pufferfish a dangerous delicacy?

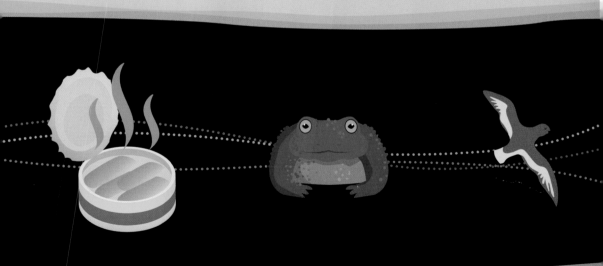

OCEANS

Most of the water on Earth is salt water, which is found in the ocean. We think of Earth's ocean as five separate oceans, but they are all connected.

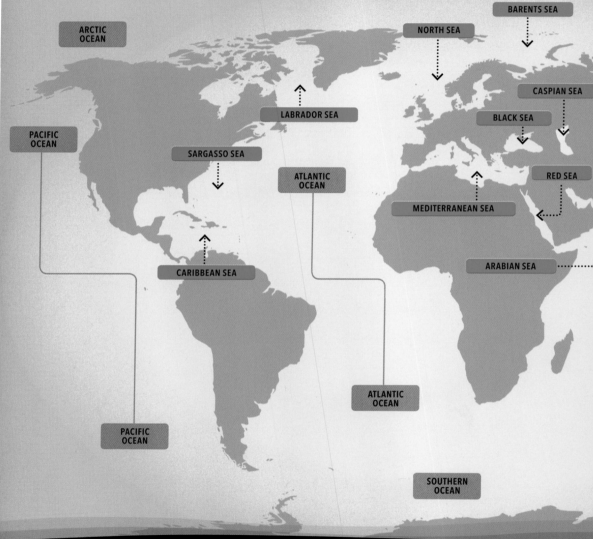

ARCTIC OCEAN

NORTH SEA

BARENTS SEA

CASPIAN SEA

LABRADOR SEA

BLACK SEA

PACIFIC OCEAN

SARGASSO SEA

ATLANTIC OCEAN

RED SEA

MEDITERRANEAN SEA

CARIBBEAN SEA

ARABIAN SEA

ATLANTIC OCEAN

PACIFIC OCEAN

SOUTHERN OCEAN

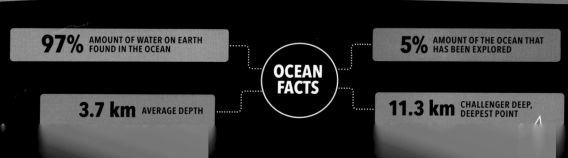

97% AMOUNT OF WATER ON EARTH FOUND IN THE OCEAN

5% AMOUNT OF THE OCEAN THAT HAS BEEN EXPLORED

OCEAN FACTS

3.7 km AVERAGE DEPTH

11.3 km CHALLENGER DEEP, DEEPEST POINT

SEAS

Seas are smaller areas of the ocean and are often near to land. There are many more seas than oceans.

BERING SEA

SOUTH CHINA SEA

INDIAN OCEAN

JAVA SEA

TASMAN SEA

★ Challenger Deep

SEA OR LAKE?

The Caspian Sea is the largest inland sea — it is completely surrounded by land! Although it sounds like a lake, it's actually a sea, because it contains salt water. In the past, the Caspian Sea was connected to the ocean, but its connection dried up, leaving the sea behind.

OCEAN LIFE

The ocean is the largest habitat on Earth. It is home to millions of different species, including fish, mammals, invertebrates, reptiles and plants. Different animals live in different temperature water and at different depths.

OCEANS BY SIZE

PACIFIC
165,250,000
SQUARE KM

ATLANTIC
106,460,000
SQUARE KM

INDIAN
73,440,000
SQUARE KM

SOUTHERN
20,327,000
SQUARE KM

ARCTIC
14,090,000
SQUARE KM

RIVERS

Rivers transform the landscape, providing water to towns and cities and allowing us to move people and goods by ship. These are some of the largest and most important rivers on Earth.

Blue Nile

White Nile

THE MISSISSIPPI RIVER

- ★ **Location:** USA (North America)
- ★ **Length:** 3,766 km
- ★ **Claim to fame:** One of the world's busiest trading routes

THE AMAZON RIVER

- ★ **Location:** Brazil, Peru and Colombia (South America)
- ★ **Length:** 6,400 km
- ★ **Claim to fame:** The most water discharged by one river – it is estimated to carry one fifth of all the water that runs across Earth's surface

THE NILE RIVER

(Its main tributaries are the White Nile and Blue Nile.)

- ★ **Location:** Egypt, Sudan and nine others (Africa)
- ★ **Length:** 6,650 km
- ★ **Claim to fame:** The longest river in the world

THE VOLGA RIVER

* **Location:** Russia (Europe)
* **Length:** 3,530 km
* **Claim to fame:** Almost half of the population of Russia lives within its basin

THE YANGTZE RIVER

* **Location:** China (Asia)
* **Length:** 6,300 km
* **Claim to fame:** The longest river in Asia and the third longest in the world

THE GANGES RIVER

* **Location:** India (Asia)
* **Length:** 2,510 km
* **Claim to fame:** The river is holy to the Hindu religion

THE MURRAY RIVER

* **Location:** Australia (Oceania)
* **Length:** 2,530 km
* **Claim to fame:** Irrigates over 70 per cent of Australia's farmland

THE CONGO RIVER

* **Location:** Democratic Republic of the Congo (Africa)
* **Length:** 4,700 km
* **Claim to fame:** The world's deepest river

GO QUIZ YOURSELF!

69 How many oceans are there?

70 Which ocean is the furthest north?

71 Name two seas.

72 What is the average depth of the ocean?

73 How deep is Challenger Deep, the deepest point in the ocean?

74 What percentage of the ocean has been explored?

75 What is the largest ocean?

76 What is the largest inland sea?

77 Which river carries one fifth of all water that runs across Earth's surface?

78 How long is the Amazon River?

79 In which country is the Mississippi River?

80 What is the longest river in the world?

81 What is the longest river in Asia?

82 What is the deepest river in the world?

83 Which river is holy to the Hindu religion?

84 Almost half of the population of Russia lives within the basin of which river?

85 In which country is the Murray River?

MOUNTAINS

Mountains are tall, rocky areas created by movement of the crust that covers Earth's surface. Mountains often form in groups, called ranges.

FORMATION

Earth's crust is divided into sections, called tectonic plates. The plates are constantly moving because of movement in the mantle beneath them. When tectonic plates move towards each other, the crust between them is pushed upwards, forming mountains.

TALL MOUNTAINS

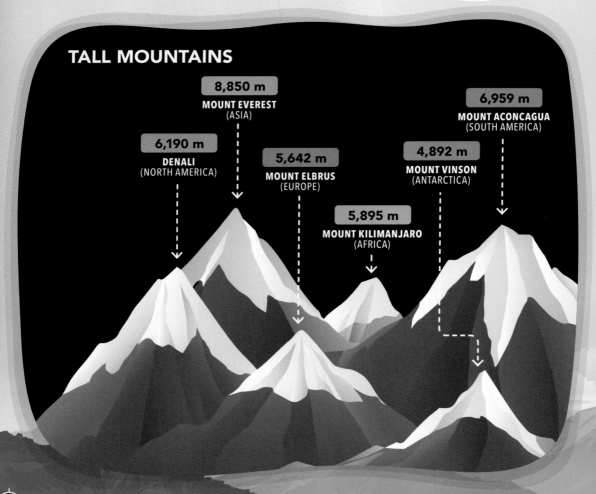

6,190 m
DENALI
(NORTH AMERICA)

8,850 m
MOUNT EVEREST
(ASIA)

5,642 m
MOUNT ELBRUS
(EUROPE)

5,895 m
MOUNT KILIMANJARO
(AFRICA)

4,892 m
MOUNT VINSON
(ANTARCTICA)

6,959 m
MOUNT ACONCAGUA
(SOUTH AMERICA)

OTHER RECORD-BREAKERS

Mount Everest is the tallest mountain on Earth when measured from sea level, but Mauna Kea, Hawaii, USA, is actually taller at over 10,000 m in total. Mauna Kea sits on the seabed, so if you measure from there to its peak, it's significantly taller than Everest!

Mount Everest

Mauna Kea

VOLCANOES

Some mountains are volcanoes. Many are active, which means that they are currently erupting or may erupt soon. Others are dormant (not expected to erupt soon) or extinct (hasn't erupted for at least 10,000 years). During an eruption, hot lava, gas and ash explode out of a volcano.

VOLCANO FACTS

★ Number of active volcanoes – 1,900

★ Number of people who live within the danger zone of an active volcano – 350 million

★ Largest volcano – Mauna Loa, Hawaii, USA

★ Most deadly 20th century eruption – Mount Pelée, Martinique, 1902 (29,000 people killed)

DESERTS

Deserts are the driest areas on Earth. They are extreme habitats, with both very high and very low temperatures. They receive almost no rain.

THE LARGEST

The Sahara Desert is the largest desert on Earth. Measuring 8.6 million square km, it's as large as the USA. It is located in the north of Africa.

THE HOTTEST

The hottest desert area on Earth is Death Valley. It is located between the Mojave Desert and the Great Basin Desert in the south of California, USA. The hottest temperature ever recorded on Earth was taken there in 1913, reaching a sweltering 56.7 °C.

THE COLDEST

Antarctica is considered a desert because it very rarely rains or snows there, and so the ice is dry. This makes it the coldest desert on Earth! Some areas of the Arctic are also deserts.

THE LEAST RAIN

The Atacama Desert in Chile, South America, receives almost no rain in some places. In 2018, some parts of the desert received rain for the first time in 500 years. Rain is so unusual there that it disrupted the balance of animals and plants in the area and caused a lot of damage.

DESERT ANIMALS AND PLANTS

Desert animals and plants have adapted to the extreme conditions in different ways.

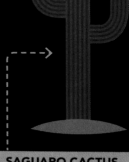

SAGUARO CACTUS

The saguaro cactus has pleats that allow it to expand to fill up with extra water during periods of rain. It stores the water to use during dry periods.

FENNEC FOX

Excess body heat from the fennec fox escapes through its large ears, cooling it down.

EAST AFRICAN ORYX

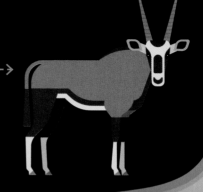

If water is hard to find, the oryx can survive on moisture from the plants that it eats or by licking dew off rocks.

86 What is a tectonic plate?

87 What is the tallest mountain on Earth, when measured from sea level?

88 On which continent is Denali?

89 What's the tallest mountain in Europe?

90 Which mountain is technically taller than Mount Everest?

91 What does it mean if a volcano is extinct?

92 How many active volcanoes are there on Earth?

93 How many people live within the danger zone of an active volcano?

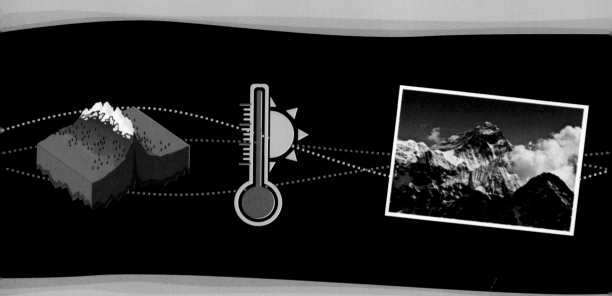

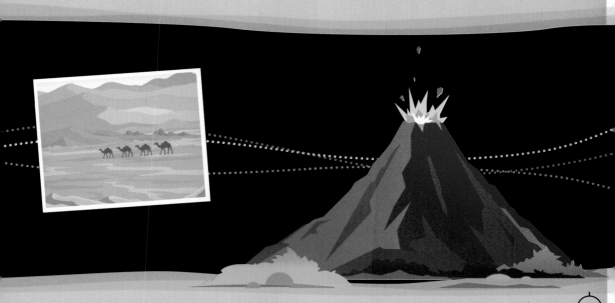

WEIRD AND WONDERFUL PLACES

We often hear about the most famous landmarks and natural areas in a country, but there are tons of strange but brilliant places that don't get the same attention. Some are natural, while others were made by humans.

PINK POND

The water of Lake Hillier, Australia, has a bright pink colour! Scientists still aren't entirely sure why the water is pink. It may be because of a reaction between a type of algae and the high salt levels in the lake.

CAT COMMUNITY

On the island of Aoshima, Japan, there are more cats than people! For every person on the island, there are six cats. The cats have total freedom to roam around and explore the island.

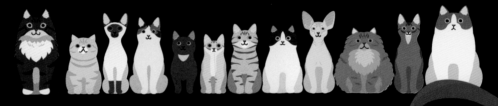

EASTER ISLAND

This island in the Pacific Ocean is also known as Rapa Nui. It is home to around 900 stone statues of heads and shoulders, known as moai. The moai probably were created to represent the spirits of their ancestors or leaders. Each statue is around 4 m tall and 12.7 tonnes in weight! They were built between the 10th and 16th centuries and still stand today.

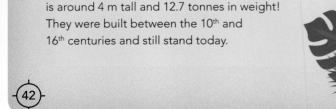

TUNNELS OF BONES

Under the city of Paris, France, is a network of 320 km of tunnels filled with the bones of around 6 million people. In the past, there wasn't enough space above ground to bury these people in cemeteries, so they placed them underground in old quarry tunnels. Later, the skulls and bones were organised in patterns to create a monument to the dead.

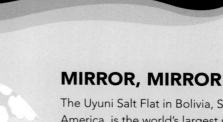

MIRROR, MIRROR

The Uyuni Salt Flat in Bolivia, South America, is the world's largest salt flat. A salt flat is created when a lake evaporates, leaving behind salt and minerals that cover the ground. This makes the ground white and sometimes reflective, making the Uyuni Salt Flat a giant mirror!

QUIZ TIME!

After you've finished testing yourself, why not use this book to make a quiz to test your friends and family? You could take questions from each section to make different rounds, or mix and match across the book for a general knowledge science quiz. You can even make up your own quiz questions! Use these weird and wonderful places facts to get you started. For example, 'On which island are there more cats than people?' or 'Which lake has bright pink water?'.

ANSWERS

1	Around 70 per cent	35	370 million
2	Seven	36	Canada
3	South Sudan	37	Mexico
4	4 million	38	Costa Rica
5	7.5 billion	39	USA
6	54	40	Mexico City
7	Lesotho	41	Cold temperatures with ice and snow
8	Tanzania	42	Bison or coyote (among others)
9	Tropical and wet	43	82 km
10	Around 315,000 years ago	44	2 million people
11	The hippopotamus	45	Angel Falls
12	Asia	46	Brazil
13	10 million square km	47	Grasslands
14	Vatican City	48	Around 6 million square km
15	Italy	49	The Inca
16	The Euro	50	2,350 m
17	Ancient Greece	51	Near to water in tropical areas
18	4.7 billion	52	Ice
19	Bangkok	53	14,200,000 square km
20	Over 6,000	54	-89.2 °C
21	Cambodia	55	2.45 km
22	China and India	56	In the centre
23	8,850 m	57	Antarctica doesn't belong to any country
24	The Dead Sea	58	Armies, weapons, military bases, oil drilling
25	China	59	Because there is no light or air pollution to block the view of space
26	Australia	60	Adélie penguin, emperor penguin and others
27	15	61	Just over 7,000
28	New Zealand	62	Mandarin Chinese
29	Aboriginal Australians	63	84 per cent
30	Hawaii	64	Asia
31	Easter Island	65	2.3 billion
32	The Māori	66	Buddhism
33	Kangaroo, koala (or wombat)		
34	They lay eggs		

67 Cambodia

68 Because it is potentially poisonous

69 Five

70 The Arctic Ocean

71 The Arabian Sea, Barents Sea, Bering Sea, Black Sea, Caspian Sea, Caribbean Sea, Java Sea, Labrador Sea, Mediterranean Sea, North Sea, Red Sea, Sargasso Sea, South China Sea, Tasman Sea (among others)

72 3.7 km

73 11.3 km

74 5 per cent

75 The Pacific Ocean

76 The Caspian Sea

77 The Amazon River

78 6,400 km

79 The USA

80 The Nile River

81 The Yangtze River

82 The Congo River

83 The Ganges River

84 The Volga River

85 Australia

86 A section of Earth's crust

87 Mount Everest

88 North America

89 Mount Elbrus

90 Mauna Kea

91 It hasn't erupted for at least 10,000 years

92 1,900

93 350 million

94 Mauna Loa

95 8.6 million square km; as large as the USA

96 The north of Africa

97 Death Valley

98 56.7 °C

99 Because it rarely rains or snows there, so the ice is dry

100 The Atacama Desert

101 Its body heat escapes through its large ears, helping it to cool down

102 By getting moisture from plants or by licking dew off rocks

HOW WELL DID YOU DO?

100–102 ---> QUIZMASTER

75–99 ----> QUIZTASTIC

50–74 ----> QUIZ ON

25–49 -----> QUIZLING

0–24 -----> QUIZ IT AGAIN

GLOSSARY

algae – a very simple type of plant, such as seaweed

ancestor – a relative who lived a long time ago

civilisation – an advanced society with its own culture

climate – weather conditions

continent – one of the seven main areas of land on Earth

crust – the outer layer of Earth

diverse – including many different types

empire – a group of countries or regions that are ruled by one group

enclaved – an enclaved country is located entirely or mostly within another country

equator – an imaginary line that goes around the centre of Earth

evaporate – when a liquid heats up and turns into a gas

geology – the study of the rocks that make up Earth's surface

glacier – a large mass of ice that moves slowly

hemisphere – one half of Earth

holy – important for religious reasons

indigenous – describes people who have always lived in a place

irrigate – to water land so that crops will grow on it

invertebrate – an animal without a backbone, such as an insect or a shellfish

mammal – a type of warm-blooded animal that gives birth to live young

mantle – the part of Earth that is under the crust

native – describes a plant or animal that lives naturally in a place and has not been brought from somewhere else

peak – the top of a mountain

plateau – a large flat area of land that is above sea level

population density – the number of people who live in a specific area

river basin – the area of land in which water flows into a river

tectonic plate – a section of Earth's crust

treaty – a written agreement between countries

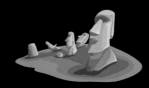

FURTHER INFORMATION

 BOOKS

Close-up Continents series
by Paul Rockett (Franklin Watts, 2016)

Continents (Infomojis)
by Jon Richards and Ed Simkins (Wayland, 2018)

Wildlife Worlds series
by Tim Harris (Franklin Watts, 2019)

 WEBSITES

kids.nceas.ucsb.edu/biomes/desert.html
Explore desert habitats and the animals and plants that live there.

www.dkfindout.com/uk/earth/continents/
Learn more about the seven continents.

www.natgeokids.com/uk/discover/geography/general-geography/ocean-facts/
Discover some amazing facts about the oceans.

INDEX